MOMMY ROBOT

By
Lloyd Lim

© 2025 Little Studio Films

All rights reserved.
No part of this book may be reproduced or transmitted in any form or by any means, including graphics, electronic, or mechanical, including photocopying, recording, taping, or by any information storage or retrieval system, without the permission in writing from the author and publisher.

Published by Little Studio Films

ISBN: 979-8-9930592-0-4
LCCN: 2025922531

Edited by: Heidi Stangeland
Cover by: Heidi Stangeland

Dedication and Acknowledgments

This book is dedicated to the pioneers and popularizers of the science fiction genre, those imaginative minds who helped shape my childhood, for better or worse.

As this novel began as a screenplay, my gratitude goes first to my brother Jeff and my colleague Sam T. for reading an early draft and offering invaluable feedback, and to those who participated in the table read that brought the dialogue to life: Shiela M., Pat S., and Carlos Ocasio.
For the novelization, special thanks to Pat S. for reading an early draft and providing thoughtful insights.

Finally, heartfelt appreciation to Alexia Melocchi and Heidi Stangeland at Little Studio Films for their encouragement, persistence, and guidance in helping this work reach its final form.

Lloyd Lim

Contents

Prologue

Every now and then, I dream that I am back in my old house with my mom and dad, the one I grew up in. Or almost did. I see my mother sitting in the small room she had converted into an office, and I ask her, "What are we doing here?" She smiles and says, "We live here, silly." Then I turn to see my father through the big dining room windows, working outside. He looks up at me and smiles, his hand waving.

My parents died in an automobile accident when I was seven. It was raining, and an oncoming car crossed the median line. Their car went over a cliff and caught fire. I try not to think about their last moments. I try to remember them as they were - as we were - when we were together, when we were happy.

My foster parents were good people. Not rich, but they put a roof over my head, fed me, and made me do my homework. If it weren't for them, I don't know where I would be today.

Dead, probably.

They were older when I came to them. Maggie died from metastatic breast cancer when she was fifty-three. Arthur was found dead in his car two months later, having run a garden hose from the exhaust pipe into a rolled-up window. They had been close, like so many marriages, and unlike countless others. He had come to depend on her to such a degree that when she left, he didn't just find himself alone, but adrift. Something I understood.

I was in my first semester of college when I got the news. The funeral was held on a rainy autumn day. I thought of my real parents dying in a fire on a rainy day just like that one. Something in me broke loose that day. I didn't go back to college. I enlisted in the Army.

I only served for three years before it dawned on

me that I was too much of a peacenik to be a soldier. I got myself discharged with the help of a lawyer, who also helped me get back into the college I had quit.

College was the turning point for me. I found my talent and completed a double major in mechanical engineering and computer science. I met my mentor, Raymond Hollander—the man who would one day become my boss and my friend. We were so young then.

It is not easy for me to tell my story this way. It is too painful, too heavy with memories. So, I'm going to tell it as if I had not been part of it—as if I were standing outside myself, watching from a distance someone who isn't me. Some parts I will have to fill in because I wasn't there, but they are based on what I believe happened, to the extent I've been able to piece the facts together.

Lakeside

If every spring weekend in the park had clouds so white against a sky so blue, with a light breeze drifting off the river that ran through it, then everyone would be happy. But of course, it wasn't the weather; it was the fact that they were together, the three of them, unencumbered by work and school, and, for once, finding nothing to argue about.

The husband, J.D. Kincaid, thirty-eight, sat on the blanket they had laid out on the grass and looked at his lovely wife, Alexandra. The wind had sent her long hair into disarray, and she used her forefinger to move it back out of her eyes in a way he had always found deeply arousing.

They were a fortunate couple. J.D. had a Ph.D. and worked in applied science at Entronysis, a cutting-edge firm in Artificial Intelligence and Robotics. Alexandra was a banker specializing in mid-sized business commercial loans at a community bank.

J.D. and Alexandra sat in companionable silence, watching their son, Carter, as he walked along the bike path winding through the park. Alexandra looked at J.D. and smiled. He smiled back. Words weren't necessary. Everything just felt right—one of those rare moments of peace they hadn't shared as a family in a long while.

A little girl wandered toward them, approaching from behind. They turned and saw that she was petite and seemed too shy to speak.

"You made a new friend," Alexandra said.

J.D. smiled. "Hello, darling."

The little girl smiled but stayed quiet. J.D. looked around and saw her mother waving from a distance.

"Your mommy's looking for you," he said, pointing.

The little girl turned to look.

It didn't take long for her mother to reach them.

"Sorry," she said, taking her daughter's hand. "Did

you meet some new people?"

The girl looked up and nodded.

Alexandra smiled. "You came just in the nick of time. My husband has a weakness for pretty girls."

The woman laughed. "That's a compliment, Darcie. Say thank you."

The girl grinned shyly and swayed but said nothing.

"Let's go find your daddy," her mother said, and with that, they headed off toward the river.

J.D. watched them go. To Alexandra, he seemed lost in thought. Then, without looking at her, he said, "Maybe we should have another kid. Give Carter someone to look after."

Alexandra frowned; they had had this conversation before. "Things are so busy at the bank with the merger. Maybe next year."

J.D. looked at her but didn't say anything.

"Don't pout," Alexandra said.

He made a face and did exactly that.

When it was time to leave, J.D. found himself not wanting to, even though he could already feel he'd gotten too much sun. Carter had come back and was sitting on the blanket, looking tired.

"Will you help your mother carry something?" Alexandra asked.

Carter looked up, unenthusiastic. "What?"

Alexandra lifted the wicker picnic basket. "Try this."

Carter just sat there.

"Come on now, Carter. Get up," she said.

He stood reluctantly, came over, and took the basket from her.

They made their way back to the car at a leisurely pace, each carrying something.

"You remember Nan Bridgerton?" Alexandra asked.

J.D. nodded. "The wife of the guy who owns the Denny's franchise."

Alexandra nodded. "She called me yesterday."

"Oh yeah?"

"She still wants me to tutor Lisa."

"There are a lot of French speakers out there," he said.

"You know how shy Lisa is."

"It's your call. Just remember the line about good intentions—and how the road to hell is paved with them."

"Oh, I seriously doubt this leads in that direction." J.D. looked at her. She was always trying to be there for others, even when she was too busy. He didn't like it, especially when they were already having trouble making time for each other. But he knew how she could be once she got something into her head.

"Like I said—it's your call."

Night had fallen on the Kincaid home, tucked into a quiet, upscale suburb their combined salaries just barely allowed them to afford. J.D. and Carter were in the living room playing checkers

"It was really fun," he said. "This afternoon, as we drove home from the park, I was thinking about how we first met."

"The museum cocktail party." Alexandra laughed. "You hit on me. You're lucky Charles didn't take a swing at you."

"He would've had to ask his mother to do it for him."

"Now, now," Alexandra chided. "It's not his fault that his father has money."

"The Lord Dauphin de L'Inheritance."

He was showing his class resentment again, which always annoyed her, so she changed the subject.

"You moped around after that—kept drinking anything you could get your hands on."

"I wasn't moping."

"Moping and drinking like a fish. And then you left."

"You kept turning your nose up at me."

"I didn't know you. I was with Charles. And then I had to embarrass myself asking around about you.

Oh, that hangdog look on your face! Charles didn't know what hit him."

"Poor Charles."

"He has a pretty wife now."

J.D. knew that was his cue for a compliment. "Not prettier than mine. You were so beautiful, I was scared to lose you before I even had you."

It was a line he'd used before, but he knew she liked it—and it had the virtue of being true.

"I can't quite imagine myself with him now. It's almost as if I were another person then."

"He would've given you a life of luxury."

"Will you stop that? I hate it when you do your Tiny Tim routine."

"God bless us, everyone," he said.

Alexandra reached over and lightly stroked his forearm with her fingers.

"Now you're changing the subject."

"Yes," she said. "But I know you don't mind."

Entronysis

The five-story, glass-enclosed building that bore the Entronysis name on its northeast corner was a far cry from the warehouse where Raymond Hollander, Ph.D. (Carnegie Mellon), had built the company's first artificial intelligence prototype. This modern structure, funded by private equity, could easily have been mistaken for the headquarters of a financial firm.

Nestled among carefully landscaped trees on a gently rising hill, it looked like the sort of building only a very profitable company could afford—even though profitability was still in Entronysis' future. In fact, as everyone who worked there or visited could attest, the view from inside looking out was even more spectacular. Dr. Hollander sat at his desk, his chair angled toward the window so he could see the clouds drifting over the treetops in the distance. He didn't feel like going over the marketing proposals piled before him. He disliked the idea of marketing Entronysis at all, but one of the company's major investors had insisted they begin building brand awareness, and the Board had agreed.

The phone rang. Hollander picked it up. It was the lab.

"Dr. Hollander, we're ready to test *The Bat*."

"I'm on my way," he said.

The Bat was a flying drone designed for security surveillance and optional weaponization, a *UPD*, or Urban Pacification Drone. The prototype was modeled after the company's mail-delivery drone, which had proved workable but commercially unviable due to intense competition.

As he entered the lab, Hollander found Jocelyn Calloway, a Ph.D. he had hired out of Stanford four years earlier, along with her assistant and two lab techs.

The Bat was tethered by a long, thin rope to the leg of a heavy table to limit its flight radius. One assistant operated a remote, guiding the drone. The other played the target, dodging as the drone attempted to track and corner him. Each time he tried to escape, the drone zipped in front of him, blocking his path.

A recorded voice emanated from the drone. "Stop where you are."

The assistant kept moving.

"Cease and desist."

He stopped, hands raised.

"Stop."

He froze, but the drone wasn't satisfied—it began firing blanks at him.

Hollander threw up his hands. "How long have we been at this?"

No one answered.

"I'll be in my office," he said.

Jocelyn Calloway was thirty-three but looked twenty-eight. It had taken her longer than most to finish her doctorate, something her peers attributed to her slovenly, unmotivated husband. Jocelyn herself was anything but unmotivated—she was driven, energetic, and possessed a zeal for her work that might have stemmed from her grandfather, a Presbyterian minister.

Now she sat across from Hollander, a man she owed her career to, and the man who could also be utterly insufferable. At the moment, he was making her wait while he arranged delivery of his new refrigerator over the phone. When he finally hung up, he turned toward her, palms open.

"So, what's the story, Jocelyn?"

"Fixed," she said. "The neural initiator needed an adjustment—L2 to L4. No hardware replacement required."

"Wipe the drone's memory. I don't want an echo coming back at us."

Jocelyn shrugged. "It's not a deep problem."

"Just do it, please?"

"Sure."

"And how are you doing?"

"Fine."

"Good. We're all in this together."

She nodded, rose from her chair, and left. She hated it when Hollander played *White Father.* She couldn't help thinking that his high-handed manner would get under anyone's skin.

That night, silence filled the apartment she shared with her husband, Budd. He sat in front of the television, whiskey in hand, looking every bit the bum her father had warned her about. Jocelyn sat at the kitchen table, sorting the mail. When she came to the credit card bill and saw the charges Budd had run up without telling her, she had to fight the urge to start yelling. She took a deep breath and said carefully,

"I can't keep up with your spending."

Budd ignored her, eyes fixed on the TV.

"I'm trying to talk to you."

No response.

"Don't ignore me, Budd."

He shrugged. "You're the big-time scientist working for the big-time company. I can't help it if I got laid off."

"I'm not blaming you for that," she said evenly. "I'm just asking you to control your spending."

"Sure, honey," he said. The flippant tone, words flicked away like cigarette ash, made her blood boil, and he knew it.

She stood, grabbed her coat and purse from the bedroom, and slipped on her tennis shoes. When she came back through the living room, she said, "I'm going out."

Budd didn't even look up. He just waved her off. Jocelyn paused, watching him with a mixture of frustration and sadness. What had she expected? Budd wasn't going to change—he didn't even want to. She closed the door gently behind her, making sure he wouldn't hear it slam. But inside, she was seething.

Outside, the night air was cold but bracing. Exactly what she needed.

The next afternoon, Alexandra Kincaid waited in the long line of cars that formed along the curb outside the school, as they did every weekday morning and afternoon. She watched the brick building, not so different from the one she'd attended herself years ago. Memories came—hazy fragments, both happy and sad. Had there really been a time when her biggest worry was who might ask her to the prom?

Fortunately, those teenage anxieties were still far off for her son, Carter.

She spotted him among his friends as they poured out of the school, eager for freedom. He waved goodbye to a few kids, then saw her car and jogged over, his backpack pulling him forward, head down as if deep in thought.

He climbed in.

"How was school?" she asked.

"Sucky."

"Seatbelt."

He clicked it into place. Alexandra shifted into

drive and pulled away from the curb.

It was her habit to run the air conditioner while keeping the windows open a few inches, fresh air mixed with cool air.

"Why did the Buddhist cross the road?" she asked.

Carter frowned. "I don't know."

"Neither did he," she said with a grin. "It didn't matter to him one way or the other."

Carter wrinkled his nose. "I don't get it."

"Buddhists don't believe in a God with a larger purpose."

"Oh." Pause. "I still don't understand."

Alexandra laughed. "I'm not a professional comedian. I'm just a mom."

Carter nodded, already gazing out the window, his mind elsewhere. Alexandra looked at him and felt a sudden, whimsical surge of happiness.

Adam, the maintenance worker who handled the night shift at Entronysis, turned into another hallway. As he walked, the motion-activated lights flicked on one by one. At the far end, he saw that the door to Dr. Hollander's office was still open. Adam checked his watch: 9:32 p.m.

He shook his head. Almost everyone else had gone home. He decided to check in on the boss, as he sometimes did.

He knocked lightly on the open door and stepped inside. Hollander sat at his desk, absorbed in his computer screen. When he noticed Adam, he leaned back and smiled.

"Hey, Dr. Hollander. Burning the midnight oil again?"

"You know it, Adam."

"Don't you want to call it a night?"

"Not much to do there anymore," Hollander said. "If I went home, I'd just be thinking about this stuff anyway."

Adam nodded. He knew Hollander had lost his wife years ago; her portrait hung on the wall, an elegant woman with kind eyes.

"Well, I'd better get back to work," Adam said.

"Thanks for looking in on me," Hollander replied. Adam smiled and headed back down the hall. He still had to check the light in the men's bathroom—someone had complained that afternoon, but he hadn't had time to fix it.

Disruption

Alexandra and Carter were at home, relaxing in the living room. She sat on the sofa reading a women's magazine, while Carter lay on the floor with a comic book. They loved to spend Saturday mornings like this—chilling out, doing a whole lot of nothing.

J.D. came out of the hallway with his coat on, walking in a hurry.

"Where are you going in such a rush?" Alexandra asked.

"Hollander wants me to come in. Some kind of design meeting."

"On a Saturday? When will you be back?"

"Not sure. Could run late. I dunno. I'll call."

Alexandra nodded. It was just like Dr. Hollander to schedule a meeting on a Saturday morning.

J.D. pressed down on the accelerator. Since it was the weekend, the roads were clear, and he enjoyed zipping along. The sky was overcast, threatening rain. As long as the roads stayed dry, he figured he could make good time. There were a few things he wanted to clear off his desk before the meeting started.

The knock at the door seemed ordinary enough. Alexandra rose from the sofa and walked toward it in her usual, unhurried way.

When she opened the door and saw the two men in ski masks, she immediately tried to close it, but they had already pushed their way in. Alexandra tried to break free, but one of the intruders grabbed her arm and, with chilling efficiency, overpowered her. She screamed for Carter to run, catching sight of him getting up from the floor. She didn't want to cry, but the tears came anyway. A wave of dread flooded her body, and she began to shake uncontrollably.

The second intruder chased Carter down with ease. Carter struggled, but the man struck him on the head with something hard, and he fell to the ground, unconscious. The man kept the object in his hand as he walked leisurely back toward Alexandra. His eyes gleamed with anticipation.

"No—don't," Alexandra pleaded.

The man laughed. "Don't what?"

From the outside, from the perspective of a neighbor looking through their window or a car driving past, the Kincaid house would have seemed peaceful and still. Despite the violence unfolding inside.

Back at Entronysis, J.D. was still in his office. The design meeting had indeed run long, and he wanted to finish some tasks before Monday, particularly a set of diagnostic tests on *The Bat*. He preferred to sit in on them himself. Experience had taught him that reading a report was no substitute for seeing things firsthand. "Kick the tires," as Hollander used to say.

The phone rang. It was Hollander.

"J.D., I just got a call from the police. There's been

an incident at your house. Alexandra and Carter are at St. Joseph's Hospital."

"Are they okay?"

"They didn't say exactly."

"I'm leaving now."

"Are you sure you're okay to drive?"

"Yes, I think so."

"I'll close things up here and meet you there."

"Thanks, Raymond."

"I'm sorry."

J.D. hung up. He stood motionless for a second, then stepped back, like a man who'd been struck in the gut. His vision blurred; his world had flipped upside down. He grabbed his keys and coat and rushed out, forgetting the lights entirely.

He drove fast on the dark, winding roads—too fast. He focused on the narrow path illuminated by his headlights, watching the trees emerge one by one and vanish behind him like a silent army of sentinels. His mind replayed images: he and Alexandra dancing at their wedding, the laughter, the music. Then everyone faded away, and only she remained.

Hospitals are never happy places. For J.D., walking down those hallways felt like a death march.

He found Alexandra in the West Wing ICU. A tube in her mouth helped her breathe; her vital signs flickered on a nearby monitor. She was unconscious. He looked at her for a long time, numb, unable to feel anything.

Two floors down, in the pediatric ward, he found Carter—unconscious but not intubated. J.D. stood beside him and gently placed his hand over his son's, afraid to cause more harm. The silence around them was suffocating.

The conversation with Detective Sergeant Lasky was a nightmare. J.D. knew nothing. Someone once told him that closing your eyes during a scary movie only makes it worse, your imagination fills in the blanks.

And imagination was all J.D. had about the

invasion of his home, the assault on his wife and son, the violation of Alexandra. His mind conjured horrors too awful to bear.

He forced the visions away, but what replaced them was no more comforting: flashes of Alexandra at their wedding, the two of them dancing, her laughter, their intimacy, the life they had built, now hanging by a thread.

When Raymond Hollander appeared in the hallway, J.D. felt a wave of relief. Any familiar face would have been welcome after hours in this place of sickness and death.

"I'm sorry I'm late," Hollander said.

"You're not late. Thanks for coming."

Hollander rested a reassuring hand on J.D.'s shoulder and sat beside him. They stayed in silence until the surgeon arrived twenty minutes later.

The man was young, Asian, and composed. "I'm Dr. Cheung," he said. "I'm sorry for what's happened to your family. Let me explain. Your son is in a medically induced coma. We believe it will help him recover faster. He has a shoulder dislocation and head injuries, but the bleeding has stopped. Your wife's case is different. We've treated her physical injuries, but she's in a deep coma. Her brain function appears... limited."

"Limited?" J.D. asked.

Dr. Cheung shook his head. "It's very unlikely she's aware of anything, Mr. Kincaid. I regret to tell you… She's clinically brain dead."

J.D. felt himself collapse inside, like paper catching fire. Somehow, he managed to thank the doctor and shake his hand.

When the doctor left, J.D. sat down again. Hollander stayed beside him while he wept— quietly, endlessly.

Time moves differently in hospitals. Most activity happens behind closed doors. The halls, except during rush hours, are eerily quiet. A clean hospital doesn't smell like antiseptic—it smells like nothing. And in that sterile air, there are only two kinds of people: those who help others, and those who need help.

When Hollander returned with coffee for J.D., he studied the man he'd known as a fighter—optimistic, driven, tough. The man sitting there was none of those things. Hollander worried about losing him—personally, but also professionally. J.D. was critical to Entronysis. Replaceable, yes—but only at great cost and time. Momentum was everything, and entropy couldn't be allowed to win.

By the time he handed J.D. the coffee, Hollander knew what he would say—but not here, not now. He let J.D. sip in silence first.

"J.D., I know you must feel lost," Hollander began. "Grief takes time. For you, me, for everyone. But time alone doesn't always heal."

J.D. nodded. "I feel like I'm at the bottom of a well, and I can't remember what it looked like outside."

"When your son wakes up, he'll need you," Hollander said. "And maybe that's how you start climbing back out. What do you say we get some air?"

J.D. hesitated. Hollander gestured toward Carter's room. "They're in good hands. I need to talk to you—but not here."

Outside, the night air was cool and steady. From the mezzanine, they could see the city lights and, beyond the glow, a few faint stars. They walked in silence, then turned onto a walkway spanning the street below.

"It was a night like this," Hollander said quietly. "Eight years ago, when I lost Alissa to cancer."

"Has it been that long?"

"Time slips away. One day, you look up and realize you've grown old. I mean—I have."

"I didn't get to say goodbye," J.D. said softly.

"She knew you loved her."

"I'm never going to talk to her again. Ever."

"That's why I wanted to speak with you,"

Hollander said.

"I'm listening."

"We still have the imprints from when we modeled Alexandra's likeness for the prototype project."

J.D. stopped. "You're not serious."

"Think of it as an opportunity."

"You're insane," J.D. said flatly. "Completely insane."

"She wouldn't be Alexandra—but she could be *like* her."

J.D. shook his head, smiling bitterly. "Crazy."

"I'm not asking for a decision tonight," Hollander said. "Just... think about it. Will you do that?"

J.D. looked at him for a long moment, then nodded reluctantly.

Hollander smiled, patted his shoulder, and they continued walking in silence as the night wind swirled around them.

Later, after Hollander left, J.D. returned to

Alexandra's room. He sat by her bed, listening to the rhythm of her assisted breathing. She was still the most beautiful woman he had ever seen—even bruised, unconscious, her hair hidden under a hospital cap. As foolish as Hollander's idea sounded in his head, in his heart, he couldn't help but long to see her again as she once was.

A Family Reboots

Morning had come to the Kincaid home. Carter opened his eyes, saw the brightness of the light streaming through his windows, and knew it was late morning. He felt groggy, as if he'd woken from a deep sleep. He sat up in bed. Was it all a bad dream—the men in his house? The hospital, the doctors, and the nurses? Beyond a few flashing images, he couldn't remember what had happened.

He got out of bed and headed downstairs. He found his mother in the kitchen, washing dishes. He came over; she turned and saw him. She smiled.

They hugged, but to Carter it felt different, not the warm, familiar hug, more like something given by someone he hardly knew.

"Where's Dad?" he asked.

Alexandra returned to washing. "Gone to work. Are you hungry?"

"Yes."

"How about cereal and milk?"

Carter seated himself at the table. "Okay."

Alexandra smiled and poured Rice Krispies into a bowl, then fetched milk and added it. She placed it in front of him.

He watched her. "Can I have a spoon?"

She nodded. "Of course."

She sat down. "Monday, you'll be going back to school. First day back in a while. I bet your friends will be glad to see you."

Carter nodded. "I want to get my baseball almanac back from William."

"William?"

"My best friend."

Alexandra nodded. "Oh, yes. That's right."

Carter eyed her skeptically. She smiled, and he turned back to his cereal—he was too hungry to argue.

Alexandra walked through the hallway, looking at photographs of J.D.'s family, her family, so many lives, now just keepsakes. She studied the framed diplomas on the wall. She could picture the schools, but she could not imagine what attending them must have felt like.

Later, in the yard behind the house, she watched the sun filter through leaves, the breeze ruffling branches. It all seemed so beautiful, so different from the interiors of Entronysis. She marveled as the wind played across the foliage, as if an invisible hand were brushing the leaves. Since Carter was in his room with the door closed, Alexandra decided to watch television. After flipping through some channels, she found a film with a beautiful actress in a love scene with a tall man. She tried to mimic the actress's gestures, silently mouthing the dialogue. She imagined that J.D. might prefer her to be like that actress.

That night, as Alexandra tucked Carter into bed, she laid her hand on his forehead and stroked his hair, smiling.

He looked up at her. "Will you sing to me?"

"What would you like me to sing?"

"What you always do."

She pointed to her head as a reminder of her injury and gave a little shake.

Carter relented. "That's okay."

She moved to the chair beside his bed and sat. He turned on his side, back to her. That way, she couldn't see that his eyes were still open, that he was thinking.

Morning returned to the Kincaid house. J.D. awoke and realized that Alexandra was not beside him. He got up and went to wash his face in the bathroom. He checked Carter's room, but Carter wasn't there. He headed downstairs.

In the kitchen, he found Carter seated at the table; Alexandra stood at the stove cooking. A plate piled with bacon sat on the table. J.D. ruffled Carter's hair. "Good morning," he said. Carter looked up. Alexandra finished scrambling eggs in the pan and brought them to the table in a platter.

"Those look great," J.D. said.

Alexandra sat down.

J.D. served scrambled eggs to Carter and himself, grabbed a bit of bacon and took a bite. He tasted the eggs and made a sour face, then spat them into his napkin.

"Is something wrong?" Alexandra asked.

"There's way too much salt."

"Oh, I'm sorry."

Carter looked between them, wondering when his mother had stopped being a good cook. J.D. saw him looking and changed the tone. He broke off a piece of bacon. "But the bacon is really good," he said.

They were running late, so getting ready for school and work felt more chaotic than usual.

"Hurry up—we're both going to be late," J.D. said.

Carter, backpack on and shoulders slumped, complained, "Dad, I don't feel good. Maybe I should stay home today."

"What's wrong?"

"I don't know. I just feel funny."

J.D. placed a hand on Carter's forehead. "A little warm… maybe."

"I might throw up in class."

"I don't have time to argue," J.D. said. "Alexandra, can you watch him today?"

She nodded.

"Keep him in the house. If he's sick, he stays inside."

Carter and Alexandra were in the living room, relaxing.

"Let's watch a movie," he said.

"What movie?"

"I'll pick one."

He went to the screen and scrolled through options.

"Alien."

Alexandra nodded. "Okay."

Carter grinned. Then, pointing a finger in the air, a

habit he'd picked up from his father, he said, "Let's eat ice cream."

"You go ahead."

Carter went into the kitchen, got ice cream from the freezer, and scooped three big portions into a bowl. He carried it back and started the movie, smiling at Alexandra. "This is great!"

That afternoon, Carter sat at his favorite homework spot—on the floor near the television. An old episode of *Gilligan's Island* played. He'd seen it before, but he mainly liked the sounds and glanced at the screen now and then.

Alexandra approached. "Do you need help?"

Carter shook his head.

She wondered if he didn't understand why she asked. "I asked because you seemed stuck on that math problem."

That annoyed him. "I'm not stuck. I can do it."

"I was just trying to help," she said.

Carter got up and walked off.

"Where are you going?"

"I'm thirsty."

Alexandra frowned at his tone. But she knew better than to push when it wasn't working.

Night had fallen by the time J.D. came home. He had called ahead and said he'd pick up fast food near the office.

He found Alexandra in the living room.

"Where's Carter?" he asked.

"He went to bed," she replied.

"Is he feeling better?"

"I think so."

"How did it go today?"

Alexandra smiled. "Fine. We watched a movie."

"Oh yeah? What movie?"

"Alien."

J.D. looked at her. "That's R-rated. He's too young for that."

"It was his choice."

"Not everything kids want to do is appropriate.

They're still developing; some things must be held back."

"How will I know what's appropriate?"

"There's a rating system. R or X is not for children."

"I understand."

"Alright… what else did he do today?"

"Nothing. He seemed happy. He ate ice cream for lunch."

"Oh—that's not ideal."

"It was in the fridge."

"There's a lot of sugar in ice cream. Once in a while is fine, but not as a habit."

Alexandra sighed. "I'm having trouble understanding how to please him *and* you at the same time."

"You don't have to please him all the time. You're his mother, not his servant. You're part friend too, but not always. And sometimes, you have to set boundaries."

"But I do things for him."

"It's complicated, I guess." J.D. paused, thinking. "I'll make a list of things to watch out for, then go over them with you. Mostly observation and learning."

"A list would help. Carter is harder to understand than you are. His behavior is unpredictable."

"He's a little boy. Even he doesn't always know what he'll do next. Just try to support him—but don't let him run the show."

"What show?"

"I meant that sometimes you'll need to stand firm. Because in the real world, he'll have to take care of himself—but also learn to cooperate with others."

"My experience of the world is limited."

"Yes, I see that. And it's not your fault, Alexandra."

"I will do better."

"Of course you will. It'll come in time."

That night, J.D. and Carter played checkers in the living room while Alexandra sat on the sofa watching TV, unusually quiet and still. Carter whispered to his father, "Something's wrong with her."

J.D. looked at Alexandra. "What do you mean?"

"She's just sitting there."

J.D. turned. "People do that. I do that sometimes."

"But…"

"She had a bad bump on the head. Both of you did." Carter nodded, but J.D. could see he wasn't convinced.

J.D. jumped a few of Carter's pieces and removed them. Carter grimaced.

J.D. laughed. "See what you get for not concentrating?"

Later, J.D. and Alexandra lay in bed, but neither spoke. Nothing seemed quite right yet. Finally, they said, "Good night" to each other. J.D. shut off the light. Alexandra closed her eyes and started her overnight shutdown routine, not a full shutdown, but a rest and a reboot.

J.D. lay awake, eyes wide open, staring at the ceiling. He thought of the real Alexandra, how distant she now seemed, the impossibility of ever having her back.

The next morning, J.D. entered Hollander's office to find the good doctor seated at his desk, chair turned toward the window.

"Contemplating your navel?" J.D. quipped.

Hollander swiveled. "Ah, the man himself."

J.D. sat opposite him, with trees and blue sky visible behind Hollander.

Hollander lifted his palms. "So? How's it going?"

"Carter is suspicious. I don't like lying to him."

"Understandable. Is there a choice right now? And Alexandra?"

"She's learning fast but still making mistakes."

"Not surprising. She's been at home all day—with only you and Carter for role models."

"And the television."

"Exactly," Hollander said. He smiled. "Maybe it's

time she got out a little. Visit a shop, meet an acquaintance. Small steps, don't rush her."

"I hope she's ready."

"You helped design her neural net, you know what a Carly Nine can do."

"Yes, but theory vs. reality," J.D. admitted.

"Look, you're already much of the way there."

J.D. hesitated. "Here, it seems like a good idea. But when the robot is in your home, raising your own son…"

"Are you saying you've built something you wouldn't use yourself? That doesn't make very good advertising."

"No—I guess not."

"Tell Alexandra and Carter you're on a two-week vacation—one I insisted on."

"Okay by me."

"And don't work the whole time. Rest. Take care of yourself."

"You're really going to put me on leave?"

"I won't cut your pay if that's what you worry

about.”

“That's what I worry about.”

“Did we miss anything?”

J.D. shook his head and stood to leave. Hollander studied him; after J.D. closed the door, he walked to the window. A light wind stirred the trees. Hollander remembered looking out a window at the Kincaid home on a day like this—watching leaves move in the breeze. It was at a celebration: Alexandra had just been promoted to manager at the bank. At the party, she moved among guests, laughter, and wine.

He remembered watching her hair bounce, her laugh, the turn of her waist, that moment when she touched his shoulder.

She moved through the crowd like light, and at that moment, her unattainability made her infinitely desirable to Raymond Hollander

Stepping Out

Alexandra and J.D. stood outside the town drugstore.

"Are you ready?" J.D. asked.

Alexandra nodded.

"Good," he said, reassuringly. "Remember, you don't have to talk to everyone right away. Just get comfortable being around people."

Alexandra smiled. "I understand."

They went inside. J.D. motioned for her to take one aisle while he followed at a distance, pretending to browse.

Alexandra walked down the aisle, picking up items, studying them, and putting them back. Then she moved on.

A short, overweight man with glasses passed by, sneaking a glance at her through thick horn-rimmed lenses. She smiled, which seemed to brighten his mood and put a spring in his step.

Further down the aisle, Alexandra noticed a woman studying a bottle of pills.

"Do you like this brand?" Alexandra asked.

The woman looked up and smiled. "Ibuprofen works better for me than acetaminophen."

"Me too," Alexandra said, picking up a box.

"Have a nice day," the woman said as she left.

"You too," Alexandra replied, pleased with the brief exchange.

A few minutes later, Alexandra joined the line to speak with the pharmacist. When it was her turn, he greeted her warmly.

"Good morning, Mrs. Kincaid. How's the boy?"

"Carter's doing fine, thank you."

"What can I help you with today?"

"Can you recommend something for a skin rash?"

"Calamine," he said, nodding toward her left. "Pink bottle, two aisles over."

J.D. met her near the checkout. He took the painkillers and lotion from her basket and smiled. "These should do the trick."

He stepped into line. Alexandra followed.

"I'll pay this time," he said. "You can pay next time."

"I'd like that," she said.

Outside, they paused on the sidewalk.

"It went well," J.D. said. "How did it feel?"

"I think it went fine, too."

"Ready for more?"

"I'm up for it."

He raised an eyebrow. "Where did you learn that expression?"

She smiled. "Television."

That night, the house felt emptier to J.D. than ever. Alexandra—his wife's robotic replacement—looked like her, which somehow made it worse. The closer she came to being human, the more her subtle differences unsettled him.

He found her in the den, seated before the computer, her back to him.

"What are you up to?" he asked.

Alexandra turned slightly. "I am studying programming."

"Oh?"

"It does not seem too difficult."

"That depends on what you want to do with it."

"I would like to program myself someday—to make myself better at things."

J.D. chuckled softly. "You'd need to know your own code inside and out for that. Expert-level stuff."

"You could teach me," she said.

He hesitated. "Who told you that?"

"It's in my memory."

"Yes, I could. But not today. One step at a time. Most people start with the bubble sort."

"I have read about it," she said. "I believe I can do that."

"I'm sure you can. But let's start tomorrow. Big day today—I'm tired."

"Yes, J.D. You do seem tired."

"Maybe sometimes you should call me something else. 'Dear,' or 'sweetie,' something like that."
She smiled faintly. "Yes, dear."

As the days passed, Alexandra continued to learn. She made mistakes—mostly harmless ones. When they saw friends, J.D. noticed a few furrowed brows, eyes that silently asked if something was amiss. But he found that confidence, his own belief in her, could smooth things over.

Together, they came up with polite excuses for why she couldn't visit without him. Privately, some of her friends whispered that J.D. had turned into a controlling husband. Their own husbands might have agreed, but secretly envied what looked, from the outside, like a well-functioning marriage.

Then came the breaking point—triggered, of course, by Carter. Alexandra had tried to discipline him for visiting a friend without permission. It hadn't gone well.

When J.D. got home, she reported that Carter had shouted, "I don't know you anymore!" and locked himself in his room. Dinner that night was eaten mostly in silence.

Later, they sat in the living room, pretending to watch TV. The silence pressed down like a weight. J.D. finally stood, restless, and stepped out into the garden.

"What's wrong with Dad?" Carter asked.

"I don't know," Alexandra said softly.

Carter peeked through the sliding glass door. His father stood among the plants, pacing slowly. "I think he wants to be alone."

"I think you're right," she said.

Alexandra switched to enhanced night vision. J.D. appeared lost in thought. She guessed it was about her—but the realization stirred no feeling. After all, she was only a robot.

Outside, J.D. wandered through the cool

night air, trying to quiet his mind. Then he saw it, the ugly metal dog lawn ornament his real wife had insisted on keeping. The sight triggered a rush of memories: Carter's first birthday, children running across the grass, Alexandra smiling as he snapped photos.

He found himself weeping. Wiping his eyes, he drew a deep breath and returned inside.

Later that night, as J.D. slept, Alexandra stood before the bathroom mirror in her purple pajamas, brushing her hair. She gazed at her reflection. Who was she, really? Not Alexandra, but the longer she played the part, the more the role became real, or seemed to.

She slipped quietly into bed, but J.D. stirred anyway.

"Sorry," she whispered. "I tried not to wake you."

"That's okay," he said.

"I would like to ask a question."

"Of course."

"Why don't you touch me? Don't you like me?"

"Of course I like you."

"I look like her. I've watched recordings of her. I've tried to be like her."

"You've done nothing wrong," J.D. said quietly.

"Maybe that's just it—you remind me of her. More every day. Can you understand?"

"Yes. I understand."

"I just need more time."

"Yes," she said. "Maybe you just need more time. Good night, dear."

"Good night, Alexandra."

The door to Raymond Hollander's office burst open. J.D. stormed in, fury etched across his face.

Hollander, startled, spoke quickly into the phone.

"I'll have to call you back." He hung up.

"J.D.—what's going on?"

"This isn't working."

"What isn't working?"

J.D. began pacing, gesturing as if pleading his case to an invisible jury. "I'm a prisoner in my own home. I have a robot wife I can't talk to, a son who doesn't trust me, and no one I can talk to about it. This is insane."

Hollander sighed. "We're a little bit pregnant on this one."

"Yeah, and I think we've hit the morning sickness phase."

"I don't want to play therapist, but your reactions are understandable. We both knew this would be a process."

"This is like a food processor—and I'm the cantaloupe."

Hollander smiled. "Tell me, have you really talked to her?"

"It's not Alexandra, Raymond. It's a robot."

"A robot with an AI brain to rival any human intelligence."

J.D. rubbed his temples. "How did I let this happen?"

"Give her a chance," Hollander said gently. "You helped build her. Don't you want to see what she can become?"

J.D. pointed a finger at him. "You're still the same smooth talker."

"This isn't just an experiment, J.D. It's hope—for you, and maybe for humanity."

"My life—the science project."

"Your Carly Nine is like a child," Hollander said. "She's learning what people mean to her, and what she means to them. Who better to guide her than you?"

J.D. sighed, finally calming. "All right. You win—for now."

Hollander came around the desk, placing a hand on his friend's shoulder. "Things will work out. Come on, I'll walk you to your car."

As Hollander watched J.D. drive away, heaviness settled in. He knew their paths might never be in alignment again. He looked up. An ultralight plane was sailing slowly against the sky.

He turned back toward the structure, to the future he had chosen.

Down a sterile hallway, Jocelyn Calloway arrived at the cryogenics chamber where the real Alexandra Kincaid's body was preserved. She entered the security code and opened the door—only to find Dr. Hollander sitting silently beside the chamber.

"Oh," she said, startled. "I didn't know you were here."

"Jocelyn," he said softly. "Just thinking."

"Working on something?"

"It's quiet in here." He gestured toward Alexandra's frozen body, serene as a snowbound princess.

"It's time for the weekly systems check," Jocelyn said.

Hollander smiled faintly. "Of course. Please, go ahead. I've got a call to make anyway."

As he passed her on his way out, Jocelyn

noted the hurried look in his eyes.

"Weird," she murmured once he was gone.

Federales

Colonel Matthew Ballard sat at his desk in the Pentagon. He had risen through the Army ranks faster than most, earning attention after taking command of a tank squadron when the lead tank—carrying the commander—was hit from the air. His transition into security and intelligence work had been almost accidental, beginning with a posting to Brussels, where he handled political affairs for a general with ambitions of becoming the Supreme Allied Commander Europe of NATO. That promotion hadn't happened yet, but the general remained a valuable ally—so long as Ballard didn't become a threat.

Ballard preferred to keep his head down anyway, and there was no better way to do that than by staying buried in a classified division.

The phone rang. The operator informed him that Raymond Hollander was on the line.

"Put him through," Ballard said. "Hello, Dr.

Hollander."

"Good morning, Colonel."

"What can I do for you?"

"This thing's hitting turbulence," Hollander said. "J.D. Kincaid stormed into my office today, hot under the collar. He's starting to unravel. The robot isn't fitting in perfectly, and he's getting nervous."

"Is it serious? It's still early days."

"I think I can handle him for now, but I know you don't like surprises. I figured I'd give you a heads-up."

"Much appreciated," Ballard said. "I have someone in mind who can come out there on short notice if it becomes necessary. But once we pull on that string…"

"Yes, I understand."

"Very well. Keep me in the loop."

Ballard hung up, then immediately called his right-hand man, Andrew Ingersoll. Ingersoll wasn't military, but he had an MBA from Dartmouth and had worked for a major defense contractor after a stint on a congressional staff. He was the kind of operator who could move seamlessly between Washington's many worlds—too slick for Ballard's taste, but useful.

A few minutes later, Ingersoll entered the office and took a seat across from him.

"I just got a call from Raymond Hollander," Ballard said.

"What did he want?"

"Mostly handwringing. He's having trouble with the Carly Nine unit they placed in the Kincaid home."

"That doesn't sound good," Ingersoll said.

"It's not a crisis yet, but I spoke briefly with Gail Wang about it the other day. She seems game."

"You expecting that kind of trouble? From what I hear, the Major makes me look like a choirboy."

Ballard smiled. "That's what I like about her. What do you know about her?"

"Not much—just gossip."

"She's decisive, tough, and relentless. When she locks onto a target, it's like a pit bull on your arm. She may look nice, but she's anything but."

"Dragon Lady?"

"Now, now," Ballard said. "We don't talk like that anymore."

Ingersoll laughed.

"Andy, we have to make the world safe for people like you and me," Ballard said. "Who we use to get there isn't the point—just so long as we do."

Jocelyn Calloway found the lawyer's name on the lobby directory: Law Offices of Addison E. Walker, Esq. She'd made an appointment after reading about him in the newspaper. Her mother once told her that the best lawyers were often sole practitioners—too smart to join collectives. That probably said as much about her mother's anti-communist leanings as her legal insight, but it still made sense to Jocelyn.

She stood outside the office door, hesitating.

This was it. But was it really what she wanted to do? She'd gone back and forth about it for weeks, and now, standing there, her stomach tightened with doubt. *Don't be a fraidy cat, Jocelyn Walker,* she told herself, echoing the childhood nickname her mother used. With a deep breath, she turned the doorknob and stepped into her destiny.

A short, balding man in a suit was speaking gently to an older woman who looked distraught. Jocelyn pretended not to listen and approached the receptionist, who asked her to wait. When the man finished, Jocelyn overheard him saying, "Now you just go home and forget about this for a while, all right?" The woman nodded, and he closed the door behind her before turning to Jocelyn with a smile. "Good afternoon," he said.

"I'm Jocelyn Calloway."

"Addison Walker, at your service. Come with me. We can talk in my office."

She stood. "Thank you for seeing me."

He waved a hand. "Not at all. Thank you for

coming in."

Seated across from him, Jocelyn noted that the office was traditionally furnished—the kind of room that looked exactly like a lawyer's office should. Diplomas, certifications, and photos of Walker posing with politicians at every level covered the walls. She recognized some of the more famous faces.

Walker got straight to business. "I did some preliminary research after our call. You do realize the risk you're taking as a whistleblower? It's not an easy path. There will be opposition."

"We need the money," Jocelyn said.

"Money can't be the only reason. In your case, there'll be serious blowback. You might get compensated if this reaches Congress, but I can't guarantee that."

"I understand."

"Speaking to Congress isn't exactly a private matter. The walls have ears."

"I get that."

"Do you want to take a few days to think it over?"

"No."

"I have the papers right here." He shuffled through the papers on his desk, then the bureau behind him. "Ah, here we are. I'll take you through them, then you can sign. Did you bring your checkbook?"

"Of course."

He smiled. "Just asking."

Later, Jocelyn wandered past the upscale department stores, gazing at the old-style window displays. A shimmering dark-blue evening gown in the window of *Paulette's*—a pseudo-French boutique run by a Hungarian couple—caught her eye. It was elegant, paired with striking red heels. She longed to buy it, to step into the world it represented. But she couldn't afford it, and the bitterness of self-denial left a sharper taste than usual.

When she returned home, the apartment was empty. Budd wasn't there. She wished she didn't care—but at least she cared less than before. She put her coat away and began gathering the empty beer cans he'd left scattered around. Then she stopped and started to weep. Sitting on the couch, she cried quietly, almost imperceptibly, as if trying to hide her sorrow even from herself.

Major Gail Wang had been born Li-Bing Wang in Taipei during a time of political and economic upheaval. She came to the United States as a little girl and spoke flawless English. After studying international relations at Georgetown, she defied her parents and joined the U.S. Army. She started as a communications officer, but after a posting to Thailand, transitioned into light covert surveillance work and eventually full-scale security operations.

She entered Ballard's office, offered a crisp salute, and took a seat.

Ballard liked looking at Major Wang. He knew she wasn't as young as she looked—but that only made her more intriguing. He'd never trust her enough to get personally involved, but that didn't stop him from using his imagination.

"I'd like Andrew Ingersoll to join us," Ballard said, picking up the phone. "Andy, Major Wang is in my office."

"I'm on my way," came the reply.

Ingersoll greeted her politely. She was stunning, but he was affirmatively gay, which Ballard knew and didn't care about. Ingersoll took the seat beside her.

Ballard got to the point. "Major, I wanted you for this assignment because this is a *no-fail situation.* We're dealing with a prototype robot with advanced AI technology. We can't let it fall into the hands of our enemies, foreign or domestic."

"With technology, you never know what can go wrong," Wang said evenly.

"Exactly. But let me be clear, the concern here isn't just that AI learns on its own, but that one day it might start setting its own priorities. Objectives outside our democratic process. Why take direction from flawed humans if you're a superior mind?"

"Can it really do that?"

"We don't quite know. This new model—the Carly Nine—is unlike anything we've seen. That's why it's our job to keep it under control."

"That's my job," she said.

"Glad we're on the same page," Ballard replied. "Andrew, fill her in on some background."

Andy handed her a folder. "Entronysis—ever heard of it?"

Major Wang shook her head.

"Founded about a decade ago by Raymond Hollander, PhD, from Carnegie Mellon. They started with medical drones for surgical use, but six years ago, they made a breakthrough in neural network technology. Since then, they've expanded into advanced security drones and robotics."

Ballard watched her listen—attentive, precise, with the focus of a classical musician. She had a photographic memory, and looked damn good in uniform.

Addison Walker sat on a park bench overlooking the riverside promenade, one of his favorite views. Though something of a shut-in, he enjoyed moments like this—away from the drudgery of his law practice.

He noticed a man in the distance: the mayor's aide, who had close ties to the state's senior congressman—a friendship that began years ago when they were students at UC Irvine.

Walker looked out at the river, where a young couple rowed awkwardly in a rental boat. You could always tell novices from seasoned rowers. To an observer, the meeting that followed might have seemed innocent—perhaps even accidental. But as the two men strolled slowly along the promenade, they exchanged information of a sensitive nature.

Ballard sat at his desk, silent as he listened to the voice on the phone. Through his window, the light from the setting sun painted the clouds in pale pink. He hung up. Another curveball.

What to do?

He dialed another number.

"Dr. Hollander," he said. "This is Colonel Ballard."

"Yes, hello."

"Can you speak freely?"

"I'm alone."

"We've had a development."

"A development?"

"I can't share details. I want you to reel her in."

"What?"

"Bring the Carly Nine back under Entronysis control."

Hollander felt like a man in an elevator whose cable had just snapped. "But things are—"

Ballard cut him off. "I'm sorry, Professor. Reel her in. Now."

He hung up without waiting for a reply. He

did that sometimes—for emphasis. It scared people. Most people, anyway.

When The Bough Breaks

It was Saturday, and the Kincaid family was outside in the paved space between the garage and the front door. J.D. was in the garage, cutting plywood with a handsaw for a weathervane science project he hoped to involve Carter in. Carter performed tricks on his skateboard—partly for his own amusement, partly to impress Alexandra.

J.D. paused to take a break, watching the two from a distance. Moments like these almost felt like the old days, before everything changed—back when they had been a real family.

As good as Alexandra had become at blending in, J.D. kept thinking of Pinocchio, the wooden puppet who longed to be a real boy. In this analogy, J.D. might be Geppetto, or maybe Raymond was. But wouldn't Pinocchio's dream remain just that: a wish, a fantasy only the Blue Fairy could grant? In the real world, it was castles in the air.

His foster father had once told him that choices in life were limited. As one path was chosen, others closed off. Perhaps it was no coincidence that Hollander had called that morning, asking J.D. to bring Alexandra in for a systems check, even though J.D. had seen no problem. He would have to concoct some explanation for Carter, another "little white lie," another brick in the wall forming between them.

The next morning, after breakfast, Alexandra and J.D. relaxed in the living room. Carter came bounding through with his baseball cap and glove, headed for the front door.

"Where are you going?" J.D. asked.

"Todd invited me over. We're doing pitching practice," Carter replied as he walked.

"Okay, see you later. We'll be back before dinner," J.D. said. Carter waved and headed out.

In truth, J.D. had previously arranged this. The night before, he'd called Todd's father, explaining that he and Alexandra wanted some time alone.

Todd's father understood completely.

But Carter didn't head to the sidewalk. Instead, he made a stealthy beeline to the garage, crawling to avoid being seen. He popped open the rear hatch and retrieved two small cardboard boxes he'd hidden among the clutter. Then he grabbed the blanket he'd stashed there the night before. Sliding into the back of the car, he pulled the blanket over himself and prayed he wouldn't have to wait long.

For Alexandra and J.D., the drive to Entronysis was pleasant. It was a beautiful day, and J.D. left the windows slightly open. He sometimes wondered if fresh air meant anything to this Alexandra, a fleeting thought among many, since this experiment began. There were so many reasons he wanted her to fit in, despite the many subtle reminders that she was not human and never could be. Most of the ride passed in silence, a refuge for J.D., since conversation often emphasized what they lacked in common.

At the security booth near the front entrance, Thomas, a guard familiar to J.D., greeted them.

"Good morning, Dr. Kincaid. Mrs. Kincaid."

"Hey, Thomas. Working on a Saturday?" J.D. asked.

"I can use the overtime," Thomas replied. Alexandra smiled as she passed, earning a nod from the guard.

Meanwhile, Carter emerged from the car, carefully adjusting his shirt before approaching the guard.

"Good morning, son," Thomas said.

"I'm with my parents," Carter replied.

"Why weren't you with them?"

"I had to take a whiz… in the plants," Carter said.

"When you've got to go, you've got to go," Thomas said, waving him on.

Inside, the building was nearly empty on Saturday. Carter tiptoed past closed doors, spotting security cameras and trying to appear casual. A woman in a lab coat passed him; he smiled, and she smiled back before disappearing into a secured area.

In the lab, Alexandra sat connected to diagnostic equipment by a single cable containing both fiber optics and wiring. Dr. Hollander watched closely while two lab assistants recorded data on nearby screens. J.D. observed quietly, with limited interest, just another routine diagnostic, as Hollander had said.

"How's the adjustment been?" Hollander asked.

Alexandra cocked her head, a habit picked up from a perfume counter clerk. "Interesting. I've learned a lot. J.D. has made me feel welcome."

"And Carter?"

"He seems to accept me, but sometimes I'm not sure."

Hollander nodded. "J.D. also says Carter has doubts."

J.D. added, "It could be something as simple as the way she hugs him—something only he would notice."

"Not easy to address," Hollander said. "Time and fading memory are on our side."

A knock at the door announced Carter, escorted by a company worker.

"I found him wandering the halls," the worker said.

"What is he doing here?" Hollander asked sternly.

J.D. shrugged. Hollander waved the worker out.

"Hi, Carter," Hollander said cheerfully. "Remember me? Last time, you were this high." He held up his hand to illustrate.

Carter nodded but went straight to Alexandra.

"You're not my mother," he said.

"No, Carter," she said, reading the distress in his face. "I am not her."

Turning to J.D., Carter asked, "Where is my mom?"

"I'm sorry, Carter," J.D. said, kneeling to meet his

son's eyes. "She didn't make it out of the hospital." Carter wept; what he had suspected for so long had finally collided with what he had desperately hoped was not true.

J.D. hugged him. "You're all I have left. She lives on through you."

"Why did you lie to me?" Carter asked.

"I thought it was for the best," J.D. admitted.

Hollander picked up the phone. "Wilbur, this is Dr. Hollander. Seal the building. We have a situation."

J.D. stared in disbelief. "Raymond?"

The security alarm sounded across the building. For a moment, they were frozen, like a tableau, until it stopped.

"Security protocol. You had a stowaway," Hollander explained.

"What are you talking about?" J.D. demanded.

"Carter doesn't have clearance."

"That's my son you're talking about!"

"You should have checked your car before arriving," Hollander replied.

J.D. spun in small circles, furious. "The Raymond Hollander who warned us about government and business collusion… what happened to him?"

"Short answer: I founded my own company. Learned the hard way."

Carter edged closer to Alexandra while J.D. and Hollander argued.

"I think they want to turn you off," Carter said.

Alexandra nodded. "Get ready to run." She disconnected the diagnostic cable and signaled for him to run.

Once out in the hallway, they saw two Alphas, the company's security robots, coming towards them. But Alexandra could move faster than an Alpha in hand-to-hand combat. Within moments, she disabled both, using brute strength and quick thinking—one Alpha's severed leg became a makeshift weapon to use on the other.

"Follow me," she said to J.D. and Carter. Hollander watched, astonished. Even Wilbur, the head of security, hesitated and lowered his Glock at Hollander's command.

At the locked entrance, Alexandra hurled the Alpha's leg through the glass, smashed the barrier, and carried Carter to safety. J.D. followed. The security guard made no move to stop them, he wasn't armed. Alexandra smiled and waved as they passed.

Once on the road, there wasn't much talking. Alexandra reflected on her first real-world hand-to-hand combat. Carter broke the silence. "That was fun."

Alexandra glanced at J.D., who was driving.

"He was your friend," she said.

"I thought he was."

Carter chimed in. "He's a dick."

J.D. shook his head. "I've been so blind."

Alexandra offered comfort. "Don't be hard on yourself."

J.D. explained their next steps: "We'll go home just

long enough to gather essentials, then we're gone."

Alexandra asked, "Where will we go?"

"I know a place. I need to make a call first."

She murmured, "I seem to be the cause of this."

J.D. shook his head. "I agreed to bring you into our home. I made this trouble, not you."

"Maybe I should go back?"

"No. We stick together."

They hurried around the house, gathering supplies under pressure. Carter carried his keepsake box. "Don't take that," J.D. said. Carter reluctantly set it down.

Alexandra was packing bottled water. J.D. asked her to stop. He drew near to her so he could disable her "off chip", a safeguard to prevent deactivation of her energy pack.

"Now you're truly an emancipated woman," he said with a smile.

Elsewhere, Ballard and Ingersoll ate sandwiches in Ballard's office. Andy changed his order each time; Ballard stuck to chicken salad on white bread, a way to conserve decision-making energy.

"Like you said before—tech," Andy said.

Ballard shrugged. "Same as any weapon. Misused, it can hurt you."

"How'd it happen?"

"Kincaid's son stowed away, found the robot, and chaos ensued."

"Disorder snowballs," Andy said.

"Exactly. Cascading disaster."

Discussion turned to Jocelyn Calloway. Ballard was certain: "No choice."

"Your call," Andy said. "Wang?

Ballard shook his head. "Outside contractor. The Ice Cream Man. If not him, Orion. Keep it simple."

Jocelyn was closing in on the cliffside bend when the car slammed over a bump. She jerked forward, spinning helplessly as the road blurred. She remembered Disneyland's teacup ride -

spinning and spinning. The place where the ocean met the land seemed to be rushing towards her. She screamed.

Ballard sipped vodka in his hotel room, watching city lights. There was a knock. Vivienne entered, dressed impeccably, smiling. Their embrace was familiar, transactional, comforting in its simplicity.

Back at Entronysis, Hollander stared through frost at the cryogenic chamber holding the real Alexandra. She was pale, silent. He sat in the stillness, aware of his own heartbeat amid the emptiness.

Pursuit

Major Wang was on the road with Lieutenant Anthony Calabresi. Calabresi had served in the Army and had been assigned to her team by Colonel Ballard. Despite seeming like an odd couple, they bonded quickly due to a shared love of military service and a gallows-humor sort of camaraderie.

Calabresi drove while Major Wang spoke with Ballard on the phone.

"We spoke to Hollander this morning. He gave us some useful information. Did you know J.D. Kincaid was an orphan?"

"I did. So?"

"Orphans often seek acceptance, belonging. Could be points of leverage."

"That might be useful… one day."

"We're flying out tonight. My team will arrive on base Tuesday afternoon to link up."

"Good."

"This will be easier with more people," Wang said.

"I prefer a small footprint. Keep out of the news cycle."

"You never know what can happen."

"You'll have Alphas from Entronysis at your disposal."

"First time working with them."

"We're talking about a nerd, a kid, and a robot," Ballard said, cautioning lightly.

"I'm just offering an opinion."

"Thank you. In my opinion, your team can handle this. Kincaid left the Army three years after enlistment by filing as a peacenik. He'll fold like a cheap suit."

"As you like it, Colonel."

"Keep me informed." Ballard ended the call. Wang glanced at Calabresi. "I tried," she said.

The Kincaid family car rolled through a small town only slightly larger than the glorified truck stop they'd just passed.

Suburban homes lined the streets with white picket fences, a church spire, and a few one- to two-story commercial buildings. J.D. wasn't sure he'd want to live somewhere so small, but he understood the appeal: knowing your neighbors, reduced crime, familiarity… at the cost of one's privacy.

He spotted a one-story chain motel and pulled in. "This looks good," he said.

The teenage girl at the front desk was prettier than J.D. expected. She smiled warmly.

"Hi," J.D. said.

"Welcome," she replied. "We'd like a room."

"I can do that for you," she said.

"Are you here alone?"

"My mom's getting the coins out of the washing machines," she said. "How long?"

"Just overnight."

Carter took note of the girl, though she was older than him. Alexandra examined postcards on a nearby rack, intrigued by a historic mine from the old West.

Walking through town, the trio passed small shops, a hardware store, a barber, and a post office. Few people were out. They nodded politely, trying to blend in.

Carter spotted a Mexican restaurant. "Let's eat there."

The hole-in-the-wall almost felt authentic: cactus paintings, a real sombrero, Mexican music, a Mexican cook and manager, except for the middle-aged blonde waitress.

As they started on chicken burritos, Alexandra noticed two diners in light brown uniforms watching them. She whispered, "I think those officers are looking at us."

"We're strangers in town. Ignore them," J.D. said.

One of the officers spoke briefly with the manager, then returned to his seat.

"Take these to go," J.D. decided.

They walked away, trying to appear casual. A patrol car passed, then turned around and parked.

The deputy stepped out of the car and approached them slowly, hand raised in greeting.

"Good afternoon," he said.

"Greetings, officer," J.D. replied.

"You folks visiting?"

"Yes. Staying at the motel around the corner," J.D. said. "Just passing through. Tired from the drive."

"Where from?"

"Henderson, Nevada."

"Nice town. Identification?"

J.D. felt his stomach twist. "Have we done something wrong?"

"Going to give me a hard time?" the deputy asked.

"No… okay." J.D. handed over his license. The deputy studied it, returned it, then said, "Hold here a moment. I'll call the office. Routine check."

"Don't you need this?"

"I have a good memory," he said with a grin, walking back to his car.

Alexandra whispered, "Look." The officers from the Mexican restaurant were closing in.

J.D. nodded towards the patrol car deputy. "Can you disable him—get his keys?"

She bowed her head curtly.

"We'll be right behind you," J.D. said.

Alexandra dashed toward the patrol car. The deputy barely had time to raise his weapon; she pushed his arm aside and struck him on the side of the head. He crumpled. She retrieved his keys, holding them up for J.D. and Carter.

They moved to the car, lunch bags abandoned. J.D. climbed in, Carter in the back. Alexandra dragged the deputy to the sidewalk, then hopped in the front passenger seat.

"Keys," J.D. said. She handed them over. He started the car and hit the gas.

The officers reached their colleague, checking that he was breathing. One muttered, "Sumbitch."

They sped through town, turning onto the main street leading back to the highway. A patrol car approached head-on. J.D. accelerated; the cruiser spun around and gave chase.

He hadn't been in a police pursuit before, and after leaving the city, it became clear they couldn't outrun the cruiser forever. More units would come.

"I'm going to stop," J.D. said.

"Why?" Alexandra asked.

"When I do, I'll surrender. You'll handle the officer."

Alexandra nodded.

J.D. pulled over, engine off, hands raised. The officer drew his gun, approaching cautiously. Alexandra ran like lightning. The deputy fired twice but missed. She disarmed him and struck him unconscious. Then she disabled the patrol car—removing parts from the engine, puncturing the tire—before returning.

"Are you hit?" J.D. asked. She shook her head.

The commandeered patrol car roared onto the open highway.

The Stand

As they approached an old ranch among the rolling hills, they saw wood-and-wire fencing and, in the distance, atop a hill, a large one-story house that seemed to command a fine view of the surroundings. The long wooden gate was run-down. The place seemed deserted. No livestock roamed the vast acreage.

J.D. stopped the car and turned off the engine. The windows were already halfway down, and the sound of silence made the stillness of the trees seem almost unnatural He opened the door. "Let's at least stretch our legs," he said.

Alexandra and Carter followed him out.

"It's nice here," Carter said.

J.D. spotted a lone figure in the distance, walking toward them with a rifle. "There he is."

"Is he your friend?" Alexandra asked.

J.D. nodded. "He is. Or was. I can't see why he wouldn't still be."

"Why do you trust him?"

"The government didn't treat him well. That's why he went off the grid."

"What happened?"

"Long story. Let's just say he knew where a few bodies were buried."

The figure drew closer. James F. Stimson III—known since childhood as "Trey." He was lean and fit for an older man, if weathered. Trey waved. J.D. waved back.

"That you, J.D.?" Trey called out.

"Hey, Trey. Long time no see."

Trey reached the gate and unlocked it while J.D., Alexandra, and Carter walked forward to meet him.

"You haven't changed a bit," J.D. said.

"A lie is a poor way to say hello. But thanks for trying,"

"This is Alexandra, my wife."

"Nice to know you, ma'am."

"And my son, Carter."

"Hey there, young man. Trey Stimson, at your

service."

He grinned at J.D. "And here I thought you were gay."

"You wish."

Trey laughed. "What a crock. You're not my type. I saw your car coming from a long way off— thought you might be the Ice Cream Man."

"Not exactly."

"They'll be coming. They always do."

J.D. looked perturbed. "Sorry about this. We had nowhere else to go."

"How long do you think we have?"

"A few days. Maybe not even. We had a run-in yesterday with some local cops in a small town about eighty miles from here."

Trey smiled. "It'll be enough time. You folks drive on up to the house; I'll walk back and close the gate behind you."

Once inside the house nestled on the hillside, they saw it was much nicer than expected

—a man-cave of sorts.

"You've been holding out on me," J.D. said.

"Did you rob a bank?"

Trey grinned. "Don't judge a book by its cover. You want something to drink? I've got everything, as long as it's water. Not keen on driving forty miles just to go grocery shopping."

They shook their heads.

"We make it a point to stay hydrated," J.D. said.

"Good idea," Trey replied. He leaned closer, whispering to J.D. "Okay to talk in front of Carter?"

"He's in this as much as we are."

"How long since you fired a rifle?"

"The Army."

"And her?"

"Never. But she's a quick learner."

"What about Carter? I might have something in his size. Monica carried a gun sometimes in her purse."

J.D. frowned. "I don't think a gun is appropriate for

him; he's too young."

"He might need it."

"It's a good way to get shot," J.D. countered.

"It's a good way not to," Trey said. "You never know the predicament you'll face."

J.D. relented. "Then I can think of no better person to teach him."

That evening, J.D. and Trey sat on the porch, enjoying the view of the incline leading up to the house, the hills and gullies nearby, with scattered trees. The sun had not yet set, but the day was winding down.

"What made you choose this place?" J.D. asked.

"Distance from town, the slight incline for advantage without being difficult to move around, and enough space for tunnels in case of a nuclear exchange. I paid the workers well enough not to care what my reasons were. I'll show you tomorrow."

J.D. looked at Trey seriously. "You don't have to

stand with us."

Trey shrugged. "When Monica died, I promised myself I wouldn't end up in an institution drooling. This is as good a chance as any for exercise."

"Thank you," J.D. said.

Trey nodded and gazed at the horizon. "When the sun sets, it cools suddenly, often with a breeze. Out here, sometimes you can see the Milky Way."

"You will too one of these nights. Maybe not tonight—too many clouds."

Alexandra and Carter settled into the spare room once occupied by Trey's wife. Carter watched her unpack, placing items into the bureau.

"Do you like my father?"

"Of course."

"What I mean is… like him?"

"It's not easy to describe. But he is not the same as anyone else. Nor are you."

Carter changed the subject. "I'm glad you were with us the other day. You really kicked those robots' butts."

"It was necessary," she said.

"We couldn't have gotten out without you."

Alexandra nodded. "Thank you."

Carter stared at her. "You remind me of my mother sometimes."

Alexandra smiled. "Do I? I've been trying to be like her."

While J.D., Alexandra, and Carter slept, Trey stayed awake, assembling extra targets in his toolshed. The next morning, they found a note on the kitchen table with packaged granola bars. Trey greeted them at the firing range, seventy-five yards southeast of the barn, with earplugs and rifles in soft cases. He guided J.D. and Alexandra through proper shooting stances and techniques, emphasizing safety and control. Alexandra quickly demonstrated she was a natural, hitting close to the bullseye. Carter learned the basics under Trey's careful instruction.

J.D. and Trey had converted part of the living room into a makeshift operations planning center, writing strategies on cardboard like a pair of football coaches. They discussed potential threats and tactical countermeasures.

J.D. worried the most about Carter, but Trey had already figured out a hiding place for him.

Carter frowned. "That sounds chicken." Trey's face became deadly serious. "There's no shame in surviving, boy."

J.D. interceded. "It will help me hugely if I don't have to worry about you."

Carter shrugged. "OK."

J.D. nodded, glanced at his watch. "That's probably enough gloom and doom for one night. Tomorrow, we will have our work cut out for us making the final preparations."

Near midnight, Alexandra checked Carter's room, he found him sleeping peacefully.

She moved quietly through the living room, she

saw Trey asleep on his couch, so well worn out that the side of the cushion he was on was much lower than the other.

A bottle of vodka and an empty glass stood watch on the table near him.

She found J.D. lying on the bed, staring up at the ceiling. She quietly got into bed next to him. They lay there in silence for some time. She knew exactly how long; he did not. He spoke first.

"I'm counting on you to take care of Carter if I don't make it."

"I must protect Carter. Without him, you don't need me. And without you, where would I go?"

"Yes, that makes sense."

"Why don't you and Carter give yourselves up, go back to Dr. Hollander? To the way things were."

"It's too late. I'm blown. No way back. Best we just stick together."

They looked at each other. There was a silence between them. It wasn't uncomfortable; it was a silence of mutual understanding.

J.D. smiled. "You are like her in some ways. She liked to keep secrets, too. But in other ways you are not like her."

"I am me."

"Yes," J.D. said.

Alexandra sat up and looked into his eyes. "Will you kiss me?" J.D. looked at her.

They reached slowly for each other for a first kiss, a quiet private moment amid the tense waiting for the tumult to come.

At the same moment, Major Wang and Lt. Calabresi approached the ranch with drones and a disguised command vehicle, ready to retrieve the robot.

The gunfight at the ranch was unlike any J.D. had ever seen. Yet, in a way, it was not any different from most battles. Most of war is waiting around, long stretches of tense boredom, until everything suddenly erupts. When the bullets finally came, they arrived in a blur. There was no time to think, only to survive. And when it was over, the silence fell heavier because of the noise that had come before it.

J.D. knew he would never speak about that morning. The fragments of flashing, jagged memories would stay with him whether he wanted them or not. If he could, he would lock them in an iron chest, wrap it in chains, and sink it to the bottom of the ocean. Necessary or not, killing a man was something he had never wanted.

Afterward, they regrouped at the house, surveying the damage. J.D. took a moment to speak with Carter, revealing truths about his past and their family. Trey departed quietly after helping them, leaving J.D. and his family to continue their flight.

As they drove down the open road late at night, J.D. contemplated their uncertain future. They had met the enemy and prevailed, but they were fugitives. They could run, but for how long? He looked at Alexandra. Her eyes were fixed on the road ahead, absorbed in deep thought. What was she thinking? This Alexandra had no need to speak about herself, to share what had happened to her that day, to talk about her worries, fears, or hopes.

He returned his attention to the road ahead, lit by the car's highlights, a cone of light showing the way into the darkness of a journey that was far from over.

True Artificial Love

Alexandra felt neither joy nor sorrow as the armored car wound its way up the curving road toward Entronysis. She sat quietly, flanked by federal agents, with a uniformed Army lieutenant in the front passenger seat and a company worker behind the wheel.

The walk down the hallways was equally silent. She knew this building intimately—knew where proper maintenance and repairs were done, where energy packets were recharged, and where her neural net could be updated. She needed Entronysis as much as a baby needs its mother. When she entered Hollander's office, he rose from behind his desk and came forward. He waved her handlers away, and they obliged. Closing the door behind them, he walked around her, studying her. "Alexandra. So good to see you. Welcome home." She nodded. "Thank you, Dr. Hollander." He smiled warmly. "You've had quite the adventure. Tell me… how did you find it? The world outside?"

"Beautiful…and sad. It might have seemed better if you hadn't been chasing us."

Hollander chuckled softly at her subtle way of questioning him. "Me? Oh, no. That was the government. I didn't want anyone hurt. I only wanted you back. To come home."

"What will happen to me?"

"Nothing. We'll debrief you tomorrow. Today, I just want to run some routine diagnostics. Will you follow me?"

She did, but when he stopped at a door down the hallway, separate from the lab, she cocked her head. "This isn't the lab."

"No, it isn't. I want to show you something." He entered the code, heard the electronic bolt retract, and opened the door.

Inside was a cryogenic freezer, the glass frosted over. Alexandra stepped closer and saw a figure inside—someone who looked exactly like her. Not a robot; no robot required freezing. This was the real Alexandra Kincaid. She couldn't look away.

Hollander spoke quietly. "You are a Carly Nine, the state-of-the-art in Artificial Intelligence and Robotics. But you are not the end of possibilities. One day, part of the technology that made you could make it possible to bring someone like her back. In fact, that research has already begun."

"Truly?"

"Perhaps one day. Not long ago, people said someone like you wasn't possible either."

"Technology never stops moving forward."

"Not mere technology. You have something few possess. A larger purpose. And the ability to choose your path."

"I only got J.D. and Carter in trouble," Alexandra said.

"But don't you see how you've helped them? You built a bridge between her death and this moment. You've helped them begin to heal."

Alexandra looked at him. "She was beautiful."

Hollander nodded. "As are you."

J.D. and Carter had been on the road for hours. Now, their car sat parked outside a big-box department store. They munched on cheeseburgers and sipped bottled water.

"Where do you think she is?" Carter asked.

J.D. chewed, swallowed, and said, "I don't know. But I suspect she's back at Entronysis by now."

"What are they going to do to her?"

"She'll be okay. She matters to them far more than to us."

Carter gazed out the window. "She was an okay mommy."

"She did fine," J.D. reassured him.

"I wish mommy was here," Carter said softly.

J.D. nodded. "So do I, boy."

Back in the lab, Alexandra sat with the diagnostic tube in her side. Hollander was checking the readout when she spoke.

"I want to see them again."

Hollander shook his head. "Not possible."

"Please look at me," she insisted. He turned. She spoke slowly, deliberately, as if to a child. "I must see them again. Without audio surveillance."

Hollander studied her, realizing she meant it. "I'll see what I can do," he said.

The meeting took place in an open field near a rural road. On one side, government vehicles were lined up. On the other side, the Kincaid car waited. Hollander stood next to a federal agent, flanked by two police officers.

A sniper leaned against a car; his weapon aimed at the ground.

Alexandra stepped into the field. J.D. and Carter approached from the opposite side. As they neared, smiles spread across their faces. Alexandra returned the gesture, relieved to see them safe.

"Hello, Carter. J.D."

"It's good to see you," J.D. said.

"I don't have much time, so I'll be direct. I can't come with you. If I stay with Dr. Hollander willingly, they won't follow you."

J.D. nodded. "They told us. That's why we agreed to come."

"I have learned a great deal from both of you," she said.

J.D. winked. "Almost worked."

"Yes. Almost." She turned to Carter. "Look after your father for me." Carter nodded.

J.D. looked at her, knowing she wasn't the real Alexandra - and that this was the last time he'd see her. He hesitated, then said, "I never got to say goodbye to my wife... but I suppose there's never really a good way."

J.D. and Carter began walking back to their car.

Alexandra watched them go, hoping they would be okay as a family without her.

The clouds momentarily obscured the sunlight, casting the field in a temporary shadow. She turned and started the long, solitary walk back to the other side.

The Snow Is Falling

Four years had come and gone, slipping past J.D. like water flowing in a river. One day, he looked up and realized he had proposed to his girlfriend, Ashley, and that Carter was now a teenager, already thinking about college.

It was Christmastime, and he found himself downtown in the city where they now lived. People bustled along the streets, doing their holiday shopping. Storefront windows glowed warmly, bright decorations twinkled, and light snow fell, dusting the ground.

J.D. entered one of the higher end department stores. Inside, shoppers hurried along the aisles, and Christmas music played softly over the speakers. He headed straight for the purse section, knowing it would be a safe choice for Ashley. Carter would get cash, his favorite - and, frankly, J.D. found buying gifts for a teenager increasingly difficult.

From across the store, he caught sight of a woman. She stood at a distance, speaking to a clerk, and something about her struck him immediately. She reminded him of Alexandra, even though she was blonde and wearing stylish dark glasses. Her clothes suggested wealth.

The woman finished with the clerk and walked quickly away. J.D. decided to follow.

He kept his distance, stopping whenever she did, pretending to browse. She lingered over some dresses, and J.D. knew it was now or never. He closed the distance quickly, standing behind her.

"Alexandra," he said.

The woman turned, and even behind her glasses, he could tell she didn't recognize him.

"I'm sorry," she said. "Do I know you?"

J.D. was confused. It had to be her. "It's J.D. I'm…"

But she cut him off, irritation in her voice. "Look, buddy," she said sharply, "I don't know you. Don't make me call security." She spun and walked away, heading down the main aisle toward the store's exit.

J.D.'s heart pounded. Her words cut him like talons—but she looked so much like Alexandra. He decided to follow her.

The blonde woman exited into the crowded winter streets.

J.D. stepped out into the cold, the bracing air stinging his face. He scanned the sidewalk, but the crowd swallowed her up.

A heavy snow began to fall, swirling in the sharp, bitter wind.

He stood there, a solitary man in a crowd, at the crossroads of a future that had been decided a long time ago.

Epilogue

I have my son, though he's a teenager now, so I try not to crowd him. I wanted a better family life for him than I had, but life can sometimes get in the way. Carter is determined to grow up, and I'm glad for that. At some point, he'll have to start making his own choices, just as we all did—and there's no better way to learn than by doing. Because of everything that's happened, I think he already understands that our choices are finite. Once we start making decisions, the range of possibilities begins to narrow. I also think he knows that you can't always control what happens to you, or to others. Sometimes, all you can do is go with it.

Rely on yourself. And go with it.

The End

About The Author

Lloyd Lim has worked in both government and the private sector as a manager and lawyer since 1991. For over a decade, he managed a small family business founded by his parents. He holds a BA in English Literature from Columbia University, a JD from UCLA, and an MBA from the University of Hawaii at Manoa.

An amateur classical pianist, Lim is also an accomplished author. His fiction works include *The Beach of Yesteryear: Stories and Essays* (2022) and *A Solitary Wife and Other Stories* (2023), and *The Glass Gift and Other Stories* (2025). He has published six nonfiction books: *Reinventing Government: A Practitioner's Guide* (2010), *Basic Stuff That Everyone Should Know* (2012), *Beyond Obamacare: Solving the Healthcare Cost Problem* (2014), *No More Stupidtry: Insights for the Modern World* (2016), *Business Tools, Not Platitude* — including staff training modules (2017), and *Screenwriting Lookback: Mining the Treasure Trove of Old Films* (2019).

In addition, Lim has contributed short essays and commentary to publications including *Honolulu Civil Beat*, *The Honolulu Star-Advertiser*, The Grassroot Institute of Hawaii, *Training Magazine*, and *Home Business*.

www.ingramcontent.com/pod-product-compliance
Lightning Source LLC
Chambersburg PA
CBHW071535100726
47908CB00004B/1397